Se
KE

J|F

RISING STARS

D1343794

9 39825739

nasen
Helping Everyone Achieve

NASEN House, 4/5 Amb[...]
Amington, Tamworth, Sta[...]

Rising Stars UK Ltd.
7 Hatchers Mews, Bermon[...]
www.risingstars-uk.com

Text and design © Rising Stars UK Ltd.
The right of Helen Chapman to be identified as the author of
this work has been asserted by her in accordance with the
Copyright, Design and Patents Act, 1988.

Published 2011

Cover design: Burville-Riley Partnership
Illustrations: Bill Greenhead for Illustration Ltd. / iStock
Text design and typesetting: Geoff Rayner
Publisher: Gill Budgell
Publishing manager: Sasha Morton
Editorial consultants: Lorraine Petersen and Dee Reid
Editorial: Jane Wood

British Library Cataloguing in Publication Data.
A CIP record for this book is available from the British Library.

ISBN: 978-184680-972-9

Printed in the UK by Ashford Colour Press Ltd, Gosport, Hampshire

MIX
Paper from
responsible sources
FSC www.fsc.org   FSC® C011748

CONTENTS

MEET THE GANG-STARS!

Jacky

Tom

Natalie

Zeke

Aaron

?

Callum

Becca

5

Claire

Name:
Tom

Special skill:
Plays the drums –
as loudly as possible!

Good at:
Drumming

Not so good at:
Reading

Other info:
Has a pop punk band called
Chasing Trouble. His younger sister
Natalie couldn't be more different.
He's good at drums – and she's good at
everything else!

PROFILES

Name:
Jacky

Special skill:
Plays piano, violin and
cello and even the
double bass…

Good at:
Being the star performer

Not so good at:
Not being the star performer

Other info:
Loves the *Last Night of the Proms* and
André Rieu. Has wanted to be a classical
music superstar ever since she started
learning the violin – at the age of three!

ABOUT ALL

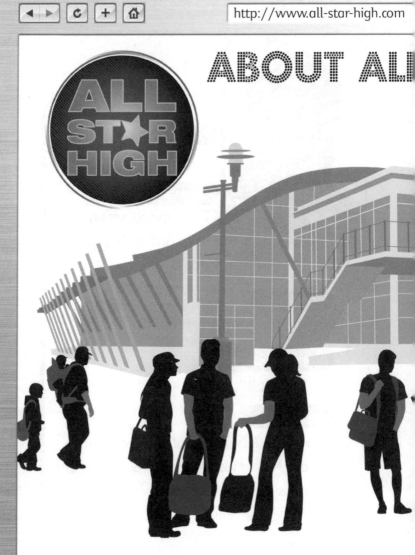

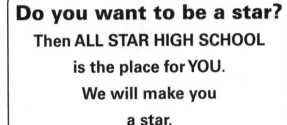

Do you want to be a star?
Then ALL STAR HIGH SCHOOL
is the place for YOU.
We will make you
a star.

Musicians,
dancers,
actors:
come see us now!

Don't miss out!

CHAPTER

Today was the worst day of Tom
Caplan's life. Tom had a pop punk band
called Chasing Trouble. At least,
he used to have a band called
Chasing Trouble. But Taz, the

double bass player, had just left the band and Chasing Trouble would be rubbish without a double bass player. Now they would never win the Battle of the Bands. It really was the worst day of Tom's life. Tom had to think fast.

Tom stood outside Music Room B. On the door there was a notice:

KEEP OUT.
THIS MEANS YOU!

'No, it doesn't,' thought Tom.

Inside Music Room B was Jacky Singh. She was playing her violin.

Classic Fest was in one week and her solo had to be perfect. Jacky wanted to win, and nobody was going to get in her way.

What Jacky didn't know was that somebody would get in her way. And that person was Tom. Tom walked into the room and slammed the door behind him.

'This is the worst day of my life,' he said. 'I don't know what to do.'

Jacky took no notice. She went on playing her violin. Tom tried again.

'I'm talking about the kind of day you wouldn't wish on your worst enemy,' he said.

But Jacky went on playing.

She wished Tom would get the hint and GO AWAY, but Tom didn't get hints. He sat down at the drum kit and picked up the drum sticks.

Jacky stopped. 'Oh no! NO WAY! You're not going to start drumming in here,' Jacky said.

'I'm having a really bad day,' said Tom. 'Taz has left Chasing Trouble. I don't have a double bass player any more and it's the Battle of the Bands next week.'

'What has a battle got to do with music?' asked Jacky.

Tom pulled a piece of paper out of

his pocket.

'Here,' he said.

'I'm busy,' said Jacky. 'Just tell me what it says.'

Reading was not Tom's thing. Reading out loud was really not his thing.

'Battle of the Bands is a competition,' he said. 'Look'.

Jacky made the paper as flat as she could. It was a poster. She read:

ROCK UP
and
ROCK ON

at the
BATTLE OF THE BANDS

All bands welcome.

Sign up NOW!

When:
28th February, 4:00 – 5:15 p.m.

Where:

 Music Hall, All Star High

Prizes:

Judge's Prizes and **People's Choice Award**

'I've already signed up,' said Tom. 'But how can I play without a double bass player?'

'Why don't you ask one of the Gang-Stars to help?' asked Jacky.

Tom and Jacky were both in the Gang-Stars. The Gang-Stars always helped each other. They had first met at an under-12s Music Club. It was so great to meet up again at high school that they started a gang.

'Like who?' Tom asked.

Jacky thought about the other Gang-Stars. 'Like… um…' she said.

Then she said, 'Yeah, you're right. No-one else plays a **string instrument.**'

Tom looked at Jacky's violin.
Of course! If Jacky could play the violin
then she could play the double bass.
Jacky was the answer to his problem.
But now he had another problem.
How was he going to get her to join
Chasing Trouble?

CHAPTER

Tom knew it wouldn't be easy to get
Jacky to join his band.

'You're a great violin player,' he said.
'You'd be an even better double bass
player in Chasing Trouble.'

Jacky just laughed. 'No way!'
she said. 'Yesterday you said I didn't
know anything about **pop punk.**
Now you want me to play in
your band!'

'I didn't need your help yesterday,'
said Tom. 'But I do now. The Battle of
the Bands is next week.'

'So is Classic Fest,' said Jacky.

'*Sick* Fest?' he said. 'Now that
is weird.'

'CLA-ssic Fest,' said Jacky.
'Not Sick Fest. Look.' She pointed to a
poster on the wall.

CLASSIC FEST

All classical players welcome.

Sign up NOW!

When: 28th February 5:30 – 7:00 p.m.

Where: Music Hall, All Star High

Prizes: Judge's Prizes and People's

Choice Award

Tom looked at the poster. It was
hard to read. The letters were muddled
up and his brain couldn't work out
the words.

'What's it about?' he said.

'Can't you see? It's like your Battle of
the Bands, but for classical players,'
said Jacky.

'But I can't play on my own
and I can't play without a double
bass player,' said Tom. 'Chasing Trouble
is a band. I need you to play the
double bass.'

'And I need to practise my violin solo,'
said Jacky. 'Sorry.'

Tom was disappointed. But he

didn't give up. He was sure that Jacky would join his band if he could make her feel bad.

'I thought being in the Gang-Stars meant something,' he said. 'Like helping your mates. I guess I was wrong.'

He slammed the door and walked down the hall. He knew Jacky would come after him. Wouldn't she?

Jacky did feel bad. The Gang-Stars had always helped her when she needed them. And now Tom needed her. She had to do it. She made up her mind and ran after him.

She got to him just at the door of the café.

'Wait, Tom,' she called.

Tom stopped and turned around.

'I'll help,' said Jacky. 'When do I start?'

Tom grinned. He had won.

'How about now? We've got time before class.'

After the first practice Jacky was fed up. Playing the double bass was easy but playing Tom's song was hard. Jacky hated pop punk music and she hated Tom's song. It only had three **chords**! And she hated Tom's drumming because it was just so loud.

She also hated Tom's singing because you couldn't hear the words. And Jacky really hated the other kids watching them practise. They were only there to see Tom singing and drumming and she felt stupid trying to be a punk star.

'It's OK. You rock,' said Tom.

But Jacky knew that wasn't true. Only Tom rocked. Nobody cared about the double bass player, but she couldn't just walk out — the Gang-Stars didn't let each other down. How could she get out of playing in Tom's band now?

CHAPTER

Finally, Jacky thought of a good plan to get out of the band. She would mess up Tom's song so that he would ditch her. At the next practice she kept playing wrong notes.

'Sorry,' she said.

But Tom was singing and drumming so loudly that he didn't notice.

So Jacky played lots of wrong notes.

'Oops,' she said.

But Tom still didn't notice.

Jacky tried something else.

'Watch out,' she said. She spun around with the double bass...
and crashed right into Tom's drum kit.

Then Tom noticed! He stopped playing.

'Hey! You're really getting into this now,' he said. 'You're awesome, Jacky. Chasing Trouble's going to rock at the Battle of the Bands. I couldn't have done this without you.'

Jacky sighed. Her plan had made things worse as Tom wanted her more than ever now. She had to come up with another plan quickly. Jacky didn't want to let Tom down but she had to find a way to get on with her violin practice too. She really wanted to win a prize at the Classic Fest.

The next day, Jacky had another plan.

'Tom,' she moaned, 'this double bass is a bit wobbly.'

At break, she moaned,

'Tom, this double bass smells bad.'

At lunch, she moaned, 'Tom, this double bass is too heavy.'

She went on moaning all day.

By the end of the day, Tom had had enough. He wanted Jacky to play in Chasing Trouble, but she was driving him mad and he didn't want to fall out with her.

'It's OK,' he said. 'Let's just forget it. You've done all you can. I'll find another double bass player.'

But that was easier said than done. The trouble started the very next day. The new player wasn't bad. She was rubbish! But what else could Tom do? It was put up with her or pull out of the Battle of the Bands.

Jacky wanted to hear what Chasing

Trouble sounded like without her.
She had felt mean leaving Tom without
a double bass player and she felt even
worse when she heard the new girl
playing. She really was rubbish! Tom
had no chance in the Battle of the
Bands with her playing!

At break, Tom and Jacky made up
their minds. They had to talk…

32

CHAPTER

Jacky went first.

'I'm sorry. This is all my fault,'
she said.

'None of this is your fault,' said Tom.
'Forget about it.'

'No,' said Jacky. 'I can't forget about it. Listen. I've got a plan.'

Tom looked at her. There was only one day until the Battle of the Bands.

'It's too late but I'm listening,' he said.

'What if we **mash up** your song?' said Jacky. 'I'll add some classical music. It'll be great.'

'Maybe…' said Tom. 'But what about the new girl?'

'Don't worry. I'll talk to her. She'll understand,' said Jacky. 'I want to come back, if you'll let me.'

'Let you?' said Tom. 'I'd LOVE you to come back. It's our only chance!'

'Great,' said Jacky. 'We can practise at lunchtime. OK?'

'Great,' agreed Tom.

At the end of the day, a boy with spiky red hair tap-danced past Tom and Jacky.

'The notice has gone up,' he said. 'You're playing first.'

'Who was that?' asked Jacky. 'I thought I knew everyone in this school.'

Tom shrugged. 'Don't know. Don't care. But look at this. He's right. Chasing Trouble is playing first.'

BATTLE
OF
THE BANDS

3:30 p.m.
Doors open

4:00 p.m.
Welcome from Principal Blake

RUNNING ORDER
4:05 p.m.
Chasing Trouble
4:15 p.m.
R

'And I'm playing first in the Classic Fest,' said Jacky.

CLASSIC FEST

5:20 p.m.
Doors open

5:30 p.m.
Welcome from Principal Blake

RUNNING ORDER
5:35 p.m.
Jacky Singh - violin
5:45 p.m.
Sam Foster

The next day at 4:05 p.m., Tom and Jacky ran on to the stage. Tom was super excited to be in the Battle of the Bands. Jacky was super amazed that she was in the Battle of the Bands!

'Want to hear some pop punk?' Tom yelled.

Noise exploded from the **audience** as they started to play. Then halfway through the song, Jacky spun round with the double bass. She started playing the song like a piece of classical music. Tom sang and played the drums more quietly. The audience loved it. They started chanting, 'Chasing Trouble! Chasing Trouble!' as Tom and Jacky ran off stage.

At last it was time for the prizes.
Principal Blake stood on the stage
and said, 'And the winner is…'

Jacky and Tom held their breath but
they didn't get the prize. They tried not
to look too disappointed.

But the principal hadn't finished.
'The People's Choice Award goes to…
Chasing Trouble!'

'It's because you wrote the song,'
said Jacky.

'And it's because of your mash-up,'
said Tom.

At 5:20 p.m., the Battle of the Bands
audience went out and the Classic Fest

audience came in. Tom and the
Gang-Stars sat at the front.

Jacky walked on stage and bowed.
The audience clapped quietly.
Jacky played her violin solo perfectly
until… she grinned at Tom and did
a mash-up of classical and pop punk
music in the middle.

The audience was amazed.
Some people held up their phones to
record her. When Jacky finished, the
audience went wild. They did not stop
clapping for ages.

'I did it!' Jacky said happily. 'I was the
star, even if it was only for ten minutes.'

At last it was time for the prizes.

Principal Blake stood on the stage and said, 'And the winner is…'

Jacky and Tom both held their breath. But Jacky didn't get the prize. She tried not to look too disappointed.

But the principal hadn't finished.

'The People's Choice Award goes to… Jacky Singh!'

'It's because of your mash-up,' said Tom.

'It's because of you,' said Jacky. 'You gave me the idea!'

As they left the Music Hall, Jacky said, 'What shall we do for the Rock Fest this summer?'

Tom was amazed.

'You mean you want to stay in Chasing Trouble?'

'Sure,' said Jacky. 'What are mates for?'

Tom thought about what a good mate Jacky was for helping him.

'Sounds good to me,' he said. There was only one way to thank her – with a song!

'I'm going to write us a new song,' he said. 'I'll call it 'With a Little Help From My Friend.'

GLOSSARY

audience – the group of people watching a performance

chords – a group of notes that sound good when they are played together

double bass – the largest classical string instrument

mash up – mixing up different music styles in one piece of music

People's Choice Award – a prize given to the audience's favourite act

pop punk – a music style that mixes punk rock and pop

principal – the headteacher of a school or college

string instrument – a group of classical instruments which have strings, including violin, viola, cello and double bass

QUIZ

1 What is Tom's band called?

2 Who had left Tom's band?

3 Where was Jacky practising her violin?

4 What time is the Battle of the Bands?

5 What time is the Classic Fest?

6 Why did Jacky keep playing wrong notes?

7 Why did Jacky want to practise her violin?

8 What does 'mashing up' a song mean?

9 Why was Jacky amazed to be in the Battle of the Bands?

10 How did Tom know that Jacky wanted to stay in his band?

ANSWERS

1   Chasing Trouble

2   Taz

3   Music Room B

4   4:00 – 5:15 pm

5   5:30 – 7:00 pm

6   So that Tom would throw her out of his band.

7   She really wanted to win the Classic Fest.

8   Mixing up different styles of music.

9   Because she doesn't usually like or play pop music.

10 Because she wanted to plan what they could play in the next rock festival.

ABOUT THE AUTHOR

Helen Chapman is an Australian author of eighty books who has been published in the United Kingdom, the U.S.A, New Zealand and Australia. She has travelled extensively and lived in America and England and is currently living in Australia.

For further information on Helen and her books visit: www.helenchapman.com

Helen has a special friend Rose Inserra who knows what her contribution has been to the ASH series and who can never be sufficiently thanked for it.

The All Star High books are available from most booksellers. For more information or to order, please call Rising Stars on 0800 091 1602 or visit www.risingstars-uk.com